The FANTASTIC FLYING Books of Mr MORRIS LESSMORE

Written by

W.E. Joyce

Illustrated by

W.E. Joyce and Joe Bluhm

SIMON & SCHUSTER

London New York Sydney Toronto New Delhi

Morris Lessmore loved words.

He loved stories.

He loved books.

His life was a book of his own writing, one orderly page
after another. He would open it every morning and write
of his joys and sorrows, of all that he knew
and everything that he hoped for.

But every story has its upsets.
One day the sky darkened.
The winds blew and blew...

. . . till everything Morris knew was scattered—
even the words of his book.

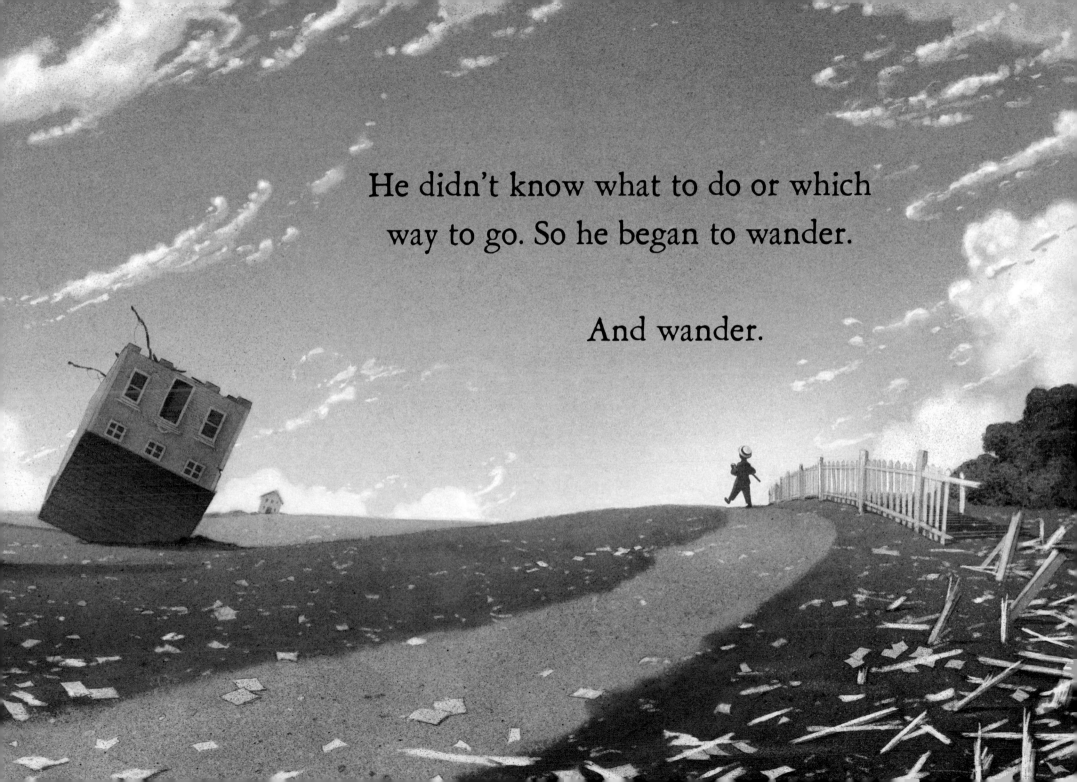

He didn't know what to do or which way to go. So he began to wander.

And wander.

Then a happy bit of happenstance came his way.
Rather than looking down, as had become his habit,
Morris Lessmore looked up. Drifting through the sky
above him, Morris saw a lovely lady. She was being pulled
along by a festive squadron of flying books.

Morris wondered if *his* book could fly.

But it couldn't.

It would only fall to the ground with a depressing thud.

The flying lady knew Morris simply needed a good story,
so she sent him her favourite. The book was an amiable fellow,
and urged Morris to follow him.

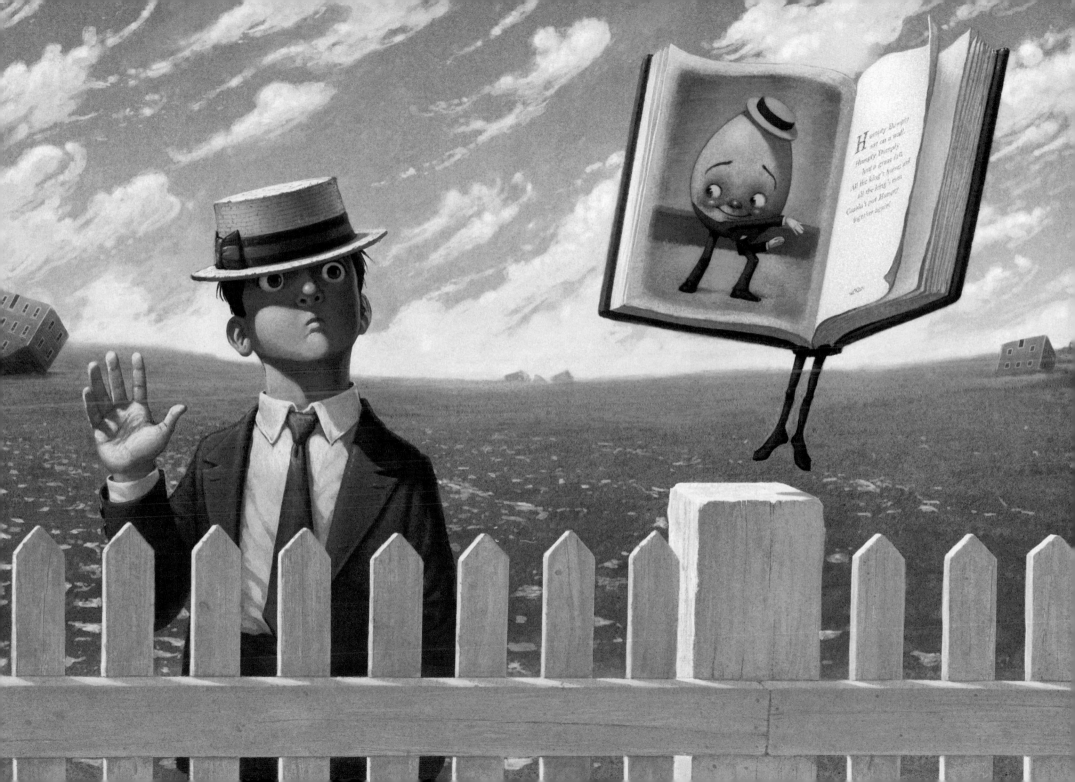

The book led him to an extraordinary building
where many books apparently "nested."

Morris slowly walked inside and discovered
the most mysterious and inviting room he had ever seen.
It was filled with the fluttering of countless pages,
and Morris could hear the faint chatter of a thousand
different stories, as if each book was whispering
an invitation to adventure.

Then his new friend flew up to him and landed on his
arm. It held itself open, as if hoping to be read.
The room rustled to life.

And so Morris's life among
the books began.

Morris tried to keep the books in some sort of
order, but they always mixed themselves up.
The tragedies needed cheering up and would visit
with the comedies. The encyclopedias, weary of facts,
would relax with the comic books and fictions.
All in all it was an agreeable jumble.

Morris found great satisfaction in caring for the books,
gently fixing those with fragile bindings
and unfolding the dog-eared pages of others.

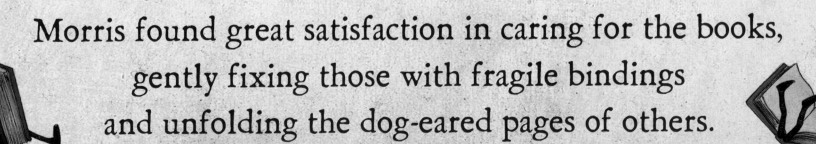

Sometimes Morris would
become lost in a book
and scarcely emerge
for days.

Les histoires ont enc[h]

Les histoires ont

histoires ont

fort que la vie et les idées qui lui

attrapée et l'ex

K

o o

y

p

Morris liked to share the books with others.
Sometimes it was a favourite that everyone loved,
and other times he found a lonely little volume
whose tale was seldom told.

"Everyone's story matters," said Morris.

And all the books agreed.

At night, after all the stories that needed telling had been told and everyone had settled down to their proper places on the shelves, the great big dictionary would get in the last word:

ZZZ Z Z Z Z Z Z Z z z z z z z z

It was then that Morris Lessmore would once again write in his own book. He wrote of his joys and sorrows, of all that he knew and everything that he hoped for.

DICTIONARY

The days passed.

So did the months.

And then years.

And years . . .

. . . and Morris Lessmore became
stooped and crinkly.

But the books never changed.
Their stories stayed the same.
Now his old friends took care of him
the way he had once cared for them,
and they read themselves to him
each night.

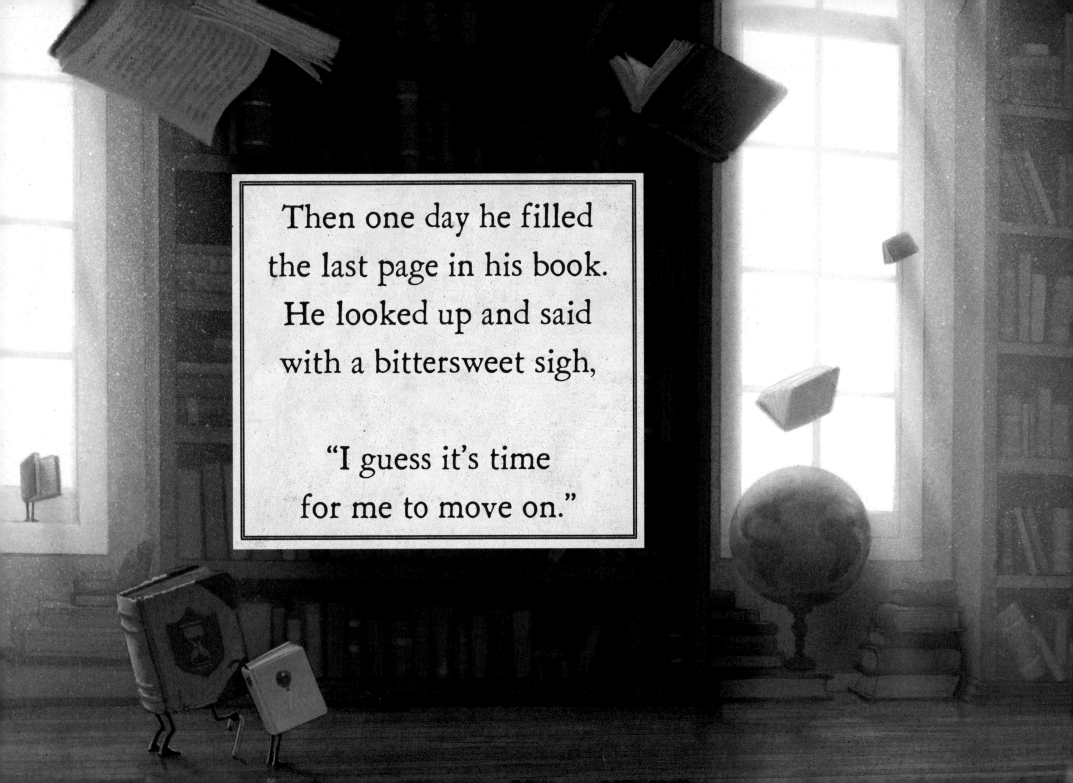

Then one day he filled
the last page in his book.
He looked up and said
with a bittersweet sigh,

"I guess it's time
for me to move on."

The books were sorry, but they understood.
Morris put on his hat and took his cane.
As he went to the door, he turned and smiled, then
waved goodbye. "I'll carry you all in here,"
he said, and pointed to his heart.

The books waved their pages, and Morris Lessmore flew away.
And as he flew, he changed back to the way he'd been
that long ago day when they'd all first met.

The books were quiet for a while. Then they noticed
that Morris Lessmore had left something behind.
"It's his book!" said his oldest friend. Inside was Morris's story.
All of his joys and sorrows,
all that he knew
and everything that he hoped for.

Then the books heard a small, expectant sound. There in the doorway was a little girl. She looked around with wonder. Then something fantastic happened.
Morris Lessmore's book flew up to her and opened its pages.

The girl began to read.
And so our story ends as it began . . .

. . . with the opening of a book.

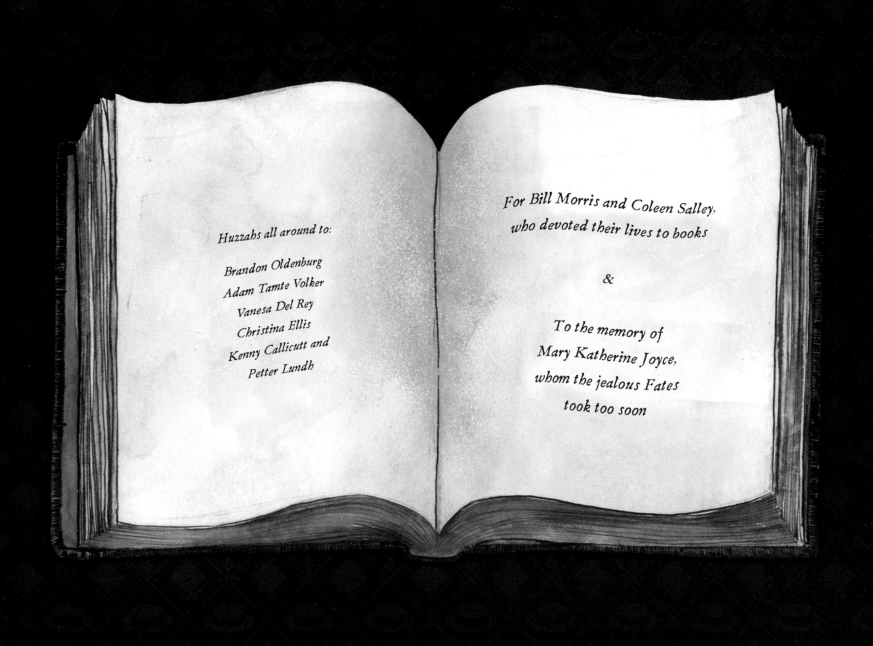

Huzzahs all around to:

Brandon Oldenburg

Adam Tamte Volker

Vanesa Del Rey

Christina Ellis

Kenny Callicutt and

Petter Lundh

For Bill Morris and Coleen Salley,
who devoted their lives to books

&

To the memory of
Mary Katherine Joyce,
whom the jealous Fates
took too soon

SIMON & SCHUSTER

First published in Great Britain in 2012 by Simon & Schuster UK Ltd

1st Floor, 222 Gray's Inn Road, London, WC1X 8HB

A CBS Company

Originally published in 2012 by Atheneum Books for Young Readers,

an imprint of Simon and Schuster Children's Publishing Division, New York

Copyright © 2012 by William Joyce and Moonbot Studios LA, LLC ®

The text for this book is set in Grit Primer.

The illustrations for this book are rendered in multimedia..

A CIP catalogue record for this book is available from the British Library upon request

ISBN: 978 0 85707 944 2

ISBN: 978 0 85707 945 9 (eBook)

Printed in China

10 9 8